Sherlock Mr Croc

Written and illustrated by
Frank Rodgers

A & C Black • London

First paperback edition 2010
First published 2009 by
A & C Black Publishers Ltd
36 Soho Square, London, W1D 3QY

www.acblack.com

Text and illustrations copyright © 2009 Frank Rodgers

The right of Frank Rodgers to be identified as the
author and illustrator of this work has been asserted by him
in accordance with the Copyrights, Designs and Patents Act 1988.

ISBN 978-1-4081-0946-5

A CIP catalogue for this book is available from the British Library.

This book is produced using paper that is made from wood grown in
managed, sustainable forests. It is natural, renewable and recyclable.
The logging and manufacturing processes conform to the
environmental regulations of the country of origin.

Printed and bound in Singapore by Tien Wah Press (Pte) Ltd.

Chapter One

Mr Croc was in the library.

"I'm looking for a book, Mrs Reid,"
he said to the librarian.

"Well, you've come to the right place,
Mr Croc," replied Mrs Reid, smiling.
"I've got thousands of books."

Mr Croc scratched his head.
"I've forgotten," he said.
(Mr Croc had a terrible memory.)

"Why don't you borrow a detective story, Mr Croc?" suggested Mrs Reid.

She picked one out for him.

It's about the most famous detective in the world, Sherlock Holmes.

Mr Croc took
the book home
and started
to read.

He liked the book so much, he read it
while making supper ...

while washing up ...

and while brushing
his one hundred
lovely teeth.

The next day, he went to see his best
friend, Mr Hound.
"I've just read a wonderful book,
Mr Hound," said Mr Croc.

Have you heard of
Sherlock Holmes?

"Of course," said Mr Hound.

8

He's the most famous detective in the world.

"Not for long," replied Mr Croc.
"Someone else is going to be *more* famous soon."
"Who?" asked Mr Hound.

Me !

Chapter Two

Mr Croc went to the shops.

He bought himself a coat, a hat and
a magnifying glass.
"To be a famous detective, you have
to look like one," he said.

He walked proudly down the street.
As he was passing the newsagent's shop,
he saw a sign.

"Aha!" cried Mr Croc. "My first
mystery!"

Mr Croc walked on. Outside the
jeweller's shop, he suddenly stopped.

There, in a crack in the wall, something
was glittering.

Aha! Maybe
it's the lost
diamond ring.

Mr Croc knelt down and peered through his magnifying glass. "No," he said.

Just then, Mrs Poodle came out of the shop. She tripped over Mr Croc's big feet, and landed ...

right on top of Mr Croc.

Her new clock flew
out of her hands and
went spinning into the
air. Down it came …

into Mr Hound's arms.

Lucky I was passing.

Mrs Poodle picked herself up. "What on earth are you doing, Mr Croc?" she said.

"Sorry, Mrs Poodle," replied Mr Croc.

"No, Mr Croc," replied Mrs Poodle, crossly.

Chapter Three

Mr Croc went on his way.
As he and Mr Hound were passing
the park, he noticed something else.

There was a glove in the hedge.

"Aha!" said Mr Croc. "Perhaps the thief left that behind."

It could be a clue.

Mr Hound started to warn Mr Croc, but it was too late.
Mr Croc grabbed the glove and pulled.

Unfortunately, the glove belonged to Mr Green, the park keeper …

and his hand was still inside it.

In a flash, Mr Croc pulled Mr Green halfway through the hedge.

"What on earth are you doing, Mr Croc?" spluttered Mr Green.

"Sorry, Mr Green," said Mr Croc.

"No, Mr Croc," replied Mr Green, crossly.

Two magpies at the top of a nearby tree called out sharply.

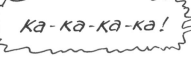

Ka-ka-ka-ka!

Lower down, a pair of squirrels made a chattering noise.

It sounded as if they were all laughing at Mr Croc.

My mystery solving isn't going very well.

"Perhaps it would be better if you put an advert in the paper," said Mr Hound.

Mr Croc rushed to the newspaper office and gave them an advert.

Mr Croc hurried
home and waited
for the phone
to ring.

He waited …

and waited …

and waited.

But nobody wanted Mr Croc to be a
detective for them.

Chapter Four

A few days later the phone *did* ring …
but it was only Mr Hound.

"The ones about the play," replied
Mr Hound. "A theatre group is putting
on a play in the town hall."

They're holding
auditions today.
Are you going?

"I don't think so," said Mr Croc.
"Someone might need a detective."

What's
the play
called?

"*Sherlock Holmes and the Mystery of the Queen's Tiara*," said Mr Hound. "I'm going!" cried Mr Croc, and rushed out of the door.

At the town hall, Mr Croc stood in line.

It looked like everyone wanted to play
the part of Sherlock Holmes.

The director gave them all a few lines
to learn.

Mr Croc smiled his lovely smile.
"I'm sure to get the part," he said to
himself. "Not only do I have the nicest
smile in the world…"

I'm also
a real
detective.

But when his turn came, Mr Croc forgot his lines ...

knocked over the scenery ...

and trod on the director's foot.

28

"I don't think you're quite right for the part, Mr Croc," said the director, hopping over to a chair.

Mr Croc turned to go.
Just then, the stage manager rushed in.
"We've had a robbery!" she cried.

The queen's tiara has vanished!

"I was washing the tiara in the next room and I left it by the open window to dry. I went away to fetch a cup of tea and when I got back it was gone!"

"Oh no!" said the director.

The mystery jewel thief has struck again!

Chapter Five

Mr Croc, the director and the stage manager hurried into the next room and stared at the empty windowsill.

The director groaned. "What are we
going to do now?" he said.

There's no
time to
order
another
tiara!

"Oh dear," sighed the stage manager.

"*Sherlock Holmes and the Mystery of the
Queen's Tiara* has turned into a real-life
mystery now!"

Mr Croc smiled his lovely smile.
"Don't worry," he said.
"I'm a detective."

I'll make your mystery history!

The director and the stage manager
shook their heads.

"It's impossible, Mr Croc," said the stage
manager.

That's right.
There are
no clues.

Suddenly, Mr Croc bent down and
picked something up.

Oh, but
there are
clues.
There are.

"Follow me!" he cried and rushed off.
The director and the stage manager
hurried after him ...

followed by the crowd outside.

Chapter Six

Mr Croc stopped at a large tree and
everyone gathered round.

"What are you doing, Mr Croc?" asked
Mrs Poodle.

Mr Croc smiled.

I'm being a detective.

Mr Green looked at Mrs Poodle.
"Oh dear," he groaned.

Not again.

But Mr Croc turned to Mr Gloss,
the painter.

Can I borrow your ladder?

Certainly, Mr Croc.

Mr Croc propped the ladder against
the tree.
As he began to climb, a pair of
chattering squirrels darted past him.

At the same time, two magpies flew past,
calling loudly.

It didn't sound as if they were laughing at Mr Croc this time. Instead, it sounded as if they were telling him to go away.

But Mr Croc didn't go away.
He kept on climbing.
The crowd held its breath as Mr Croc
disappeared among the leaves.

A few moments later he appeared again
and began to climb back down.

As he stepped off the ladder, Mr Croc smiled his lovely smile.

He took a diamond ring, a silver badge and a gold watch out of one pocket …

and the queen's tiara out of the other.

The crowd cheered.

"The magpies were the mystery thieves," explained Mr Croc.

They're attracted to bright, glittery things.

"If they spot something shiny, they pick it up when nobody's looking and take it back to their nest."

Mr Croc showed them what he had picked up at the town hall – two black-and-white feathers.

But when they stole the tiara, they left these clues behind!

The director and the stage manager were thrilled to get the tiara back.

Thank you, thank you, Mr Croc!

The show is saved!

Mrs Poodle was delighted, too.
The ring was hers.

She gave
Mr Croc
a big kiss.

"Thank you, Mr Croc," she said.

I'm sorry I called
you a nuisance.

"So am I," said Mr Green, as Mr Croc
returned his silver badge.

You're brilliant
at being a
detective.

Mr Croc held up the watch.

Who does this belong to?

"Er … I think that's yours, Mr Croc,"
said Mr Hound.

You reported it
missing last week.

Mr Croc blushed. "So I did," he said.

My goodness,
what a dreadful
memory I've got!

44

Chapter Seven

The next morning there was a picture of Mr Croc on the front page of the paper.

SHERLOCK MR CROC SOLVES MYSTERY OF QUEEN'S TIARA

A mystery surrounded the disappearance of three items

"Well done, Mr Croc," said Mr Hound.

You <u>are</u> a famous detective now.

The director was delighted, too. "What wonderful publicity, Mr Croc!" he cried.

He gave Mr Croc two tickets. "These are for the opening night. I'd like you to take a bow on stage."

"Of course," replied Mr Croc, his eyes twinkling. "After all, I'm sure the audience would love to see the most famous …

and the *second* most famous detective in the world together on the same stage."

Mr Croc smiled his lovely smile, showing all of his one hundred shiny teeth.